SUNNY and the WICKED LADY

ALISON MOORE has been writing stories since she was a child, and was first published – through a local writing competition – when she was eight. She began writing her first novel, *The Lighthouse*, the year her son was born, and recently published her fourth novel and her first book for children, *Sunny and the Ghosts*. She lives in a village on the Leicestershire-Nottinghamshire border with her husband and son and a cat called Shadow.

ROSS COLLINS was born in Glasgow, Scotland, quite a while ago. At that time he would eat anything and resembled a currant bun. Ross has written sixteen children's books and illustrated over a hundred. He no longer resembles a currant bun. He lives in Glasgow with a strange woman, a small child and a stupid dog.

ALSO BY ALISON MOORE

Sunny and the Ghosts (Salt 2018)
Sunny and the Hotel Splendid (Salt 2019)

Alison Moore

Illustrated by Ross Collins

SALT

CROMER

PUBLISHED BY SALT PUBLISHING 2020

2 4 6 8 10 9 7 5 3 1

Copyright © Alison Moore 2020

First published in Great Britain in 2020 by
Salt Publishing Ltd
12 Norwich Road, Cromer, Norfolk NR27 0AX United Kingdom

www.saltpublishing.com

Salt Publishing Limited Reg. No. 5293401

A CIP catalogue record for this book is available from the British Library

ISBN 978 1 78463 229 8 (Paperback edition)
ISBN 978 1 78463 230 4 (Electronic edition)

Typeset in Neacademia by Salt Publishing

Printed and bound in Great Britain by Clays Ltd, Elcograf S.p.A

For Arthur, Lucianne and Cara

Sometimes, a story you read or hear will be total fiction, pure fantasy, make-believe, a fabrication, a fable, a yarn. And sometimes it won't.

CHAPTER ONE

The Ruined Castle

ABOVE THE ANTIQUE, vintage and second-hand shop, breakfast was finished and Sunny was getting ready for school. When the phone rang, Sunny's mum picked it up and said, 'Hello?' After a moment, she said again, 'Hello?' She put the phone down, saying to Sunny, 'That's odd. There's no one there.'

Some hours later, in between home time and teatime, the phone rang again. This time, Sunny got there first. He picked it up and said, 'Hello?'

'Sunny!' said Elsie. 'I've been trying to reach you, but your parents keep answering and of course they can't hear me.'

Sunny, who could hear his ghostly friend just fine, asked if everything was all right, so Elsie told him that the Hotel Splendid was thriving and that she, Mary and Alan were very well, though they were missing

Abigail who was spending the week in London, haunting a West End theatre.

'Alan's been taking Mary and me to see all sorts of interesting local places,' said Elsie. 'Normally, we prefer to do our sightseeing at night-time.' All the ghosts knew the dangers of the busy daylight hours, the discomfort of being walked through or sat on by the people who could not see them. Alan had once been standing on the promenade, leaning on the railings, looking out to sea, when a man came and stood right inside him, sucking on a strawberry split that gave Alan a terrible ice-cream headache. At night-time, when people were mostly fast asleep and streets were mostly deserted, the ghosts felt safe to roam. 'We'd very much like to visit Okehampton Castle,' said Elsie, 'but it's too far to walk to so we've decided to go by bus on Sunday morning. I was wondering if you and the others would like to meet us there?'

Sunny said he would love to and that he would ask his parents. He was optimistic because Sunday was the one day of the week when the shop was always closed.

He asked at teatime, and his mum and dad said yes. His mum said she would bring a picnic, and his dad said he would bring the folding chairs, and Sunny said he would bring the ghosts.

Before bed, Sunny went down to the shop, which was currently inhabited by three ghosts. During the

day, the ghosts stayed out of the way, but at night, when they had the shop all to themselves, Herbert climbed out of his blanket box, and Walter emerged from his wardrobe, and Violet came out of the stationery cupboard. Herbert and Walter always looked forward to a night spent reading books and playing music, and Walter had started learning Spanish, and there was a new box of old board games that the ghosts were working their way through. Usually, Violet was keen to sit down at her desk and spend the hours writing, but she had recently finished editing her second book and she had not yet had an idea for a third. She was waiting for inspiration to strike.

Sunny told the ghosts about Elsie's phone call and the plan to meet at the castle on Sunday. 'Do you want to come?' he asked.

Herbert consulted his calendar and told Sunny he had the whole day free and to count him in.

'Sí,' said Walter, 'por favor.'

'I'll bring my notepad,' said Violet, 'just in case I see something I want to write about.'

On Sunday morning, while Sunny's mum and dad

were locking up the shop and getting into the van and choosing music to listen to on the way to the castle, Sunny was helping Herbert, Walter and Violet into the back. When everyone was in, they set off.

Herbert got out a book, and Violet and Walter started a game of I Spy.

'I spy with my little eye,' said Violet, 'something beginning with G.'

While Walter was looking around, trying to guess, Herbert was reading. Walter said to Herbert, 'Are you sure you should be reading that?'

'That's right, Herbert,' said Violet. 'You don't want to get travel sick.'

'You definitely don't want to get travel sick,' agreed Walter, 'but I mean, are you sure you should be reading a book of ghost stories? The last one you read really scared you.'

Herbert had in particular been frightened by the tale of the Wicked Lady who rode in a coach made of human bones. He had been convinced that she was coming after him, and even though it had turned out to be just his imagination, she still gave him the heebie-jeebies. 'I've thought of that,' said Herbert, showing them the cover of his book, which was 50 *Real American Ghost Stories*. 'These ghosts are thousands of miles away, so I ought to be safe.' He went back to his book, and did not look up until the van turned the final corner, at which point he glanced through the window and saw the sign for Okehampton Castle. 'Oh dear,' he said. When Sunny had said they would be going to a castle, Herbert had not realised which castle he meant, but now he knew. 'This is the ruined castle,' he said, 'that the Wicked Lady haunts.'

Violet peered through the windscreen at the ruins, at the stony towers and roofless walls, which went out of sight as the van entered the car park. As they pulled into a parking space, Herbert said, 'I don't feel very well.' There was a noise outside that made him jump, but it was just Sunny opening the door to let them out.

Violet was the first out of the van, with her notepad at the ready, followed by Walter, the only one of the three who *could* have gone through a *closed* door: not all ghosts could do that, but Walter had been a ghost for a long time and had learnt a few tricks.

Violet said to Herbert, 'Come and get some fresh air. You'll feel better soon.'

They walked up the lane until they came to the entrance to the castle grounds, where Elsie, Mary and Alan were waiting for them. Sunny and the six ghosts greeted one another excitedly. With Sunny's parents walking ahead and Sunny and the ghosts following behind, they explored what was left of the castle. They talked about what the castle might once have looked like – how grand it must have been, with archers in the keep, and feasts in the Great Hall – and they played hide-and-seek amongst the ruins, although Herbert was unusually quiet and did not join in with the games.

'Are you feeling any better, Herbert?' asked Violet.

'Yes, thank you,' said Herbert. But he seemed on edge and distracted.

'Is anything wrong, Herbert?' asked Violet.

'I'm just keeping an eye out for the Wicked Lady,' said Herbert.

'But Herbert,' said Violet, 'the Wicked Lady is just a story in your book.'

'Just because she's a story in a book,' said Herbert, 'doesn't mean she's not real.'

A game of tag had started, and while Violet joined in, Herbert stood watch.

When Sunny and his parents sat down to eat their picnic, neither he nor the ghosts had seen any sign of the Wicked Lady. Some of the ghosts lay down in the grass and rested in the sunshine, but Herbert could not relax.

'We've been all round the castle,' said Violet, 'and we haven't seen her. I really don't think she's here.'

'She might be biding her time,' said Herbert. 'The moment we let our guard down, she'll pounce.'

But Sunny and his parents finished their picnic and

packed everything away and still the Wicked Lady had not shown herself. 'Time to go home,' said Sunny, getting to his feet, and to Elsie, Mary and Alan he added, 'We can take you to the bus stop if you like.'

As they walked away from the ruins, Violet said to Herbert, 'See? No Wicked Lady.'

'I bet that's a relief, eh, Herbert?' said Walter.

'To be honest,' said Sunny, 'I'm a bit disappointed we didn't see her, even though she sounds quite scary.'

'The Wicked Lady is *very* scary,' said Herbert. 'I've read all about her. After marrying for money, she killed her husband. Then she married again . . . She had four husbands in total and killed them all, and . . .' He went on and on, describing all the bad and worse things she had done in her lifetime, and he recited some verse he knew about her equally alarming ghost:

> *'My ladye's coach hath nodding plumes,*
> *The driver hath no head;*
> *My ladye is an ashen white,*
> *As one that is long dead.*
> *My ladye hath a black blood-hound*
> *That runneth on before . . .'*

Somewhere nearby, a dog barked, and Herbert nearly jumped out of his ghostly skin. When he had recovered, he continued:

> '"Now pray step in," my ladye saith,
> "Now pray step in and ride."
> I thank thee, I had rather walk
> Than gather to thy side . . .
> I'd rather walk a hundred miles
> And run by night and day
> Than have that carriage halt for me
> And hear the ladye say:
> "Step in with me and ride."'

The ghosts had reached the car park now, and Herbert, with a last glance over his shoulder, was the first to get back in the van. When everyone was in, Sunny closed the door, then hopped into the front and strapped himself in. His dad pulled out of the car park and joined the end of a queue of traffic.

'I heard from Abigail this morning,' said Elsie, and four ghostly heads turned towards her to hear how Abigail was getting on in London. 'Normally,' explained Elsie, 'the theatre is haunted by the Fading Lady, but the Fading Lady's gone on holiday with the theatre manager, so Abigail agreed to take over for the week. She has to walk down this staircase . . .'

Only Herbert was not paying attention. He was looking through the back window, in the direction of the ruined castle. He rubbed his eyes and looked again, and shook his head and looked again, at the ghost with shadowy eyes who was standing in the lane, looking right at him. 'The Wicked Lady . . .' he murmured. And, at her side, her spectral black dog. As Herbert watched in horror, she began to walk briskly towards him, and her hound came too. Herbert willed the traffic to move. The Wicked Lady was getting closer. She had almost reached the back of the van, and was raising her arm, reaching for the door, for the window behind which Herbert sat frozen, speechless.

'. . . and just as she reaches the bottom step, she has to scream!' said Elsie, as the van set off and the Wicked Lady was left behind, staring after them. 'Abigail said that at first she was doing the scream too early or too late or forgot to do it altogether, but now she's got it just right. And apparently the theatre has a phantom dolphin as well, which Abigail says is very friendly.'

Violet liked the sound of the phantom dolphin, and said to Herbert, 'There's a phantom cow in your book, isn't there? Herbert?'

'The Wicked Lady,' whispered Herbert.

'The Wicked Lady?' said Violet.

'I saw her,' said Herbert, raising his arm to point through the window at the back of the van. 'She was right there. She was coming to get me.'

Everyone turned to look where he was pointing, but there was no one there.

CHAPTER TWO

The Coach of Bones

THAT NIGHT, WHEN Violet suggested playing a game of Scrabble, Walter expressed surprise. Violet loved Scrabble and always won, but she had been playing games night after night and doing no writing at all. 'Again?' asked Walter. 'Aren't you going to write?'

Violet sighed. 'I don't know what to write about,' she said.

'I expect you'll get an idea soon,' said Walter sympathetically.

Herbert did not know what to do with himself. He paced the shop, picked up a book and put it down again, sat and stood up again.

'Herbert, are you still worrying about the Wicked Lady?' asked Violet.

Herbert nodded.

'Perhaps a nice game of Scrabble will take your

mind off it,' said Violet. So they played Scrabble, which Violet won again, and then they played Monopoly, which Herbert won, and then Twister, which Walter won. When morning came and the ghosts heard getting-up noises and bathroom noises and breakfast noises coming from upstairs, they put away their games. Walter went into his wardrobe and got comfy inside the winter coat that hung there. Violet went into her cupboard. As a rule, the stationery cupboard was kept locked during the day, so Herbert locked the door behind her and put the key back in its place in the drawer in the cash desk. He was just about to climb into his blanket box when he heard a noise outside the shop: it was a clattering and rumbling noise, a clip-clopping and rolling noise, and it sounded exactly how he expected the Wicked Lady's coach of bones would sound. Herbert did not need to think twice: he ran into the hallway and up the stairs to the flat where Sunny's dad was just coming out of the bathroom. Herbert ran in behind him and climbed into the laundry basket to hide.

In the middle of the morning, while Sunny's mum

was minding the shop, a customer came in. She was heard before she was seen because her pointy-toed, spiky-heeled shoes made such a noise coming along the pavement. She wore a pale grey suit and her ash-grey hair was scraped back and fixed in a knot. She walked around the shop, pausing to admire the framed butterflies. She eyed the silk rug and said to Sunny's mum that she was sorry not to see a tiger-skin rug anywhere. 'They're such beautiful creatures,' she said. 'They make such beautiful rugs.' She stopped to look at the blanket box and asked, 'Is this the only blanket box you have?' Sunny's mum said it was. The woman lifted the lid and looked inside, then lowered the lid again and said she would take it.

'It is a lovely item,' said Sunny's mum, taking the customer to the cash desk. She made a note of the sale, writing down 'Blanket box', and the price, and the customer's name, which was Mrs Prenderghast. 'And if you give me your address,' said Sunny's mum, 'we can deliver it to you later today.'

'There's no need,' said Mrs Prenderghast. 'I can take it with me in my van. I want to get it to the museum as soon as possible.'

'You're from a museum?' said Sunny's mum. 'I didn't think the blanket box was especially old.'

'Well,' said Mrs Prenderghast, 'it's just what I want.'

Between them, they carried the blanket box outside

and loaded it into the back of Mrs Prenderghast's van. Mrs Prenderghast slammed the doors shut and, looking very pleased with her purchase, drove off, leaving behind a dark and stinky cloud of exhaust fumes.

At lunchtime, Sunny's dad came into the shop with some new old things. He stopped to look at where the blanket box had been, and asked where it was.

'I sold it,' said Sunny's mum.

'Huh,' said Sunny's dad. 'The place feels kind of strange without it, doesn't it?'

Sunny's mum nodded. 'It was just after we moved here that you brought it into the shop. And Sunny lifted up the lid and said, "Dad, there's a ghost in the blanket box!"'

'Yes, I remember that,' said Sunny's dad.

'Ah,' said Sunny's mum fondly. 'And he said the ghost was called Herbert, and Herbert lived in the blanket box.'

'Yes,' said Sunny's dad. 'Herbert will have to live somewhere else now.'

'You don't think he'll mind too much, do you?' said Sunny's mum.

'Who, Herbert?' said Sunny's dad.

'No, not *Herbert*,' said Sunny's mum. '*Sunny*. This *is* a shop, after all. These things *are* for sale. Besides, perhaps Sunny's getting a bit old for imaginary friends.'

After school, Sunny had football club, and after football club he had been invited to his friend Charlie's house for tea. Sunny always felt quite at home at Charlie's house. Charlie's mum was a historian, who gave talks in libraries and village halls, telling the stories of local places and the people who had lived there in years gone by. Charlie's house was full of old black-and-white and sepia photographs, showing streets that Sunny recognised, but instead of cars and vans there were horse-drawn carts, and the bicycles were penny-farthings; the men wore three-piece suits and the women wore long dresses and everyone wore hats, and children played with hoops and sticks. There had been a lot of change since those long-gone days, but some things in these photographs – a row of shops, a pub, a church, and trees – had been there for more than a hundred years, from one generation to the next, and were still there now.

Charlie was not very interested in history. He liked Minecraft, and Sunny did too. They played until their tea was ready, and then they played some more.

By the time Sunny got home, the shop had closed for the day, but Sunny had his own key and could let himself in. He came into the hallway just as Herbert was creeping back down the stairs. Herbert had found the laundry basket reasonably comfortable, but there was no getting away from the fact that it was full of pants, and he had greatly missed his beloved blanket box.

Seeing Sunny coming from the shop, Herbert asked if there was anyone in there. 'No,' said Sunny, 'but I expect Walter and Violet will be coming out soon.'

'No one else?' asked Herbert.

'Who else *would* be there?' asked Sunny.

'No one at all!' said Herbert brightly, going into the shop.

'Is everything all right, Herbert?' asked Sunny, following him.

Herbert was inside the shop now, looking at the bare floor. 'Where's my blanket box?' he asked.

Sunny, who had come through the shop without looking at where the blanket box wasn't, stared at the empty space where it ought to have been, as if, by looking hard enough, he could make himself see it. He went to Walter's wardrobe and opened the door. 'Walter,' he said, 'do you know where the blanket box has gone?'

Walter, who had spent the day listening to *Spanish for Beginners* on his Walkman, blinked in the sudden light and took off his headphones.

'The blanket box has gone,' repeated Sunny.

Walter came out of the wardrobe to look. 'I hope it's not been sold,' he said.

They were *all* hoping it had not been sold, but they couldn't think of any other explanation.

Violet was still inside her cupboard, but was knocking on the door, wanting to be let out. When the door was unlocked, she came out, saying, 'I really must learn how to go through doors. It would be a very useful skill to have.' She looked at her friends' sad faces and said, 'Yes, the blanket box has gone. I was terribly worried you were in it, Herbert, and that you'd been taken away. I've been shouting so much I've just about lost my voice, but no one could hear me. I'm so glad to see you're safe after all.'

'How come you weren't in the blanket box, Herbert?' asked Walter.

Herbert explained. 'This morning, at breakfast time, when you'd gone into your wardrobe, Walter, and you'd gone into your cupboard, Violet, and I was about to climb into my blanket box, I heard a noise outside the shop: I heard clattering and rumbling, clip-clopping and rolling. Do you know what it sounded like? It sounded exactly how the Wicked Lady's coach of bones would sound.'

'Oh Herbert!' said Violet. 'Not this again. It's just a story, Herbert.'

'No,' said Herbert, 'she's real and she came here this morning. I heard her coach of bones.'

'But did you actually see it?' asked Violet.

'No,' said Herbert. 'I ran upstairs and hid in the laundry basket. I've been there all day.'

'Did you see it, Walter?' asked Violet.

'No,' said Walter. 'But if she was here, she's gone now.'

Herbert nodded, looking warily around the unlit shop. 'Like my blanket box,' he said. Then, frowning, he added, 'Do you think the Wicked Lady took my blanket box?'

'Why would the Wicked Lady want your blanket box?' asked Violet.

'It's a very nice blanket box,' said Herbert defensively.

'Yes,' agreed Violet, 'it is, but the Wicked Lady didn't take it. A lady from a museum bought it.'

'A museum?' said Sunny. 'A museum wanted Herbert's blanket box?'

'Apparently so,' said Violet.

'Sunny?' His mum was calling down from upstairs. 'Is that you?' She came down to the shop.

'You've sold the blanket box,' said Sunny.

'Yes,' said his mum.

'It's lucky Herbert wasn't in it,' said Sunny. 'He'll miss it though – he's got nowhere to go now.'

'Don't worry about me,' said Herbert. 'I can find somewhere new.'

'You can stay with me in my wardrobe,' offered Walter.

'That's very kind of you,' said Herbert.

'It's going to be in a museum,' said Sunny's mum. 'I expect Herbert would be proud to know that his old blanket box was going to be on display. It must be older than we thought, or valuable in some way.'

Herbert thought about this. It *was* nice to know that someone thought his blanket box was of sufficient period interest to be displayed in a museum, but on the whole he would rather it was still in the shop.

Violet, who had not managed to get a good look at Mrs Prenderghast, asked Sunny to get a description of her. She wrote it down in her notepad, like a police officer taking down a description of a criminal.

When Sunny and his mum had gone upstairs, the ghosts got out the box of board games, but no one was really in the mood: Herbert was feeling out of sorts, and the others were feeling very sorry for him. On top of that, Violet decided that not even something as dramatic as Herbert's blanket box being sold was enough to write a book about, so she was still stuck.

They whiled away the hours until the sky grew light again. When they heard the family upstairs moving around, starting their day, the ghosts packed away their games, ready for a rest now.

Violet was just going into her cupboard, and Herbert was ready to lock the door behind her, and Walter was in his wardrobe, holding the door open for Herbert to follow him in, when Herbert said, 'Listen . . .' Walter listened. Herbert's ghostly eyes were wide with worry. 'Can you hear that?' he asked.

'I can hear something . . .' said Walter.

Violet, half in and half out of the cupboard, said, 'It's a clattering, rumbling sort of noise . . .'

'It's a clip-clopping, rolling sort of noise . . .' said Walter.

'It's the coach of bones!' said Herbert.

'It won't be the coach—' began Violet, as a ghostly coach of bones rolled into view.

'Scarper!' shouted Herbert, hurrying through the back door into the hallway and then up the stairs to the flat, with Walter close behind him. Herbert hid in the laundry basket, which was now even more full of pants, and Walter hid in the nice big wardrobe with smoothly sliding doors in Sunny's parents' bedroom.

But Violet had lingered. She had gone to the window and was gazing avidly at this coach that was made from bones and decorated with human skulls and pulled by spectral skeletal horses. It came to a stop outside the shop, like something that had travelled right out of a story. There was a door in the side of the carriage, which slowly opened. Violet watched as a ghostly foot emerged, followed by the skirt of a ghostly gown. She watched as the Wicked Lady approached the door to the shop, her shadowy eyes peering in. Violet took a step back into the safety of the shop, and then another step into the nearest hiding place, which was Walter's wardrobe, and, with her ghostly fingers trembling, she pulled the door to.

Shortly after opening time, when Sunny's mum was once again looking after the shop, Mrs Prenderghast returned. This time, she was with a young man, who accompanied her around the shop, having a good look at all the furniture.

'What about this wardrobe, Edgar?' said Mrs Prenderghast, drawing the young man's attention to the smarter of the two wardrobes: it had curlicues and a mirrored door, which he opened. But having inspected it, he shook his head. Moving on to Walter's wardrobe, the young man opened it up and peered inside. Violet shrank back behind the winter coat and held her breath. He was only just a grown-up, she

thought, looking at his face, his wispy beard. But when he looked in Violet's direction he showed no surprise, so he must, she thought, have been unable to see her.

'Yes,' said the young man, closing the door again. 'This one's perfect.'

Mrs Prenderghast turned to Sunny's mum and said she wanted to buy the wardrobe.

'For the museum?' asked Sunny's mum.

'That's right,' said Mrs Prenderghast.

'I would have thought *that* wardrobe was more suited to a museum,' said Sunny's mum, pointing at the fancier wardrobe.

'But *this* is the one we want,' said Mrs Prenderghast.

'It has a keyhole,' observed the young man. 'Is there a key?'

'I think there *is* a key somewhere,' said Sunny's mum. She went to look in the drawer in the cash desk, but it wasn't there. 'Just a moment,' she said, and left the room.

Violet, aware that it was time to get out, shifted closer to the wardrobe door. While Mrs Prenderghast was saying, 'I hope it's not got woodworm,' Violet eased the door open, to make a gap that she could just about get through. But the young man must have noticed the old hinges creaking, the door coming open, because before Violet could get even a little way out, he had pushed it to again. Sunny's mum returned with a little brass key that fitted perfectly into the keyhole and, when turned, locked the door.

Mrs Prenderghast was keen to pay and get going. As Sunny's mum wrote down the details of the sale – item, price, buyer – she thought to ask which museum Mrs Prenderghast was from. 'Is it the Museum of Dartmoor Life?' she said.

'No,' replied Mrs Prenderghast. 'It's a brand-new museum, opening next week. I'll give you my phone number. If you get any more wardrobes or blanket boxes or other interesting items of furniture, give me a call and we'll come and take a look.'

Sunny's mum said she would do that, and wrote Mrs Prenderghast's phone number next to her name in the sales ledger.

The wardrobe, nearly empty, was not too heavy, and between them they carried it out to the van. Closing the door behind them, Sunny's mum looked around at the shop, which now seemed oddly bare.

After school, Sunny came in through the shop as usual and saw straight away that one of the wardrobes was missing.

'Where's the other wardrobe?' he asked his mum.

'I sold it,' said his mum, 'to Mrs Prenderghast.'

'But that's Walter's wardrobe!' said Sunny. 'Walter will have been in it!'

'Isn't he a ghost?' said Sunny's mum. 'Can't he go through walls?'

'Yes,' said Sunny, 'he can . . .' But where was he?

And then there was Herbert, who had agreed to share Walter's wardrobe but who, unlike Walter, could not go through walls. Sunny was getting worried. He went to the stationery cupboard, hoping that he would find Herbert and Walter in there with Violet, but even Violet was not there. He called out to them: 'Herbert? Walter? Violet? Where are you?'

Upstairs, Herbert and Walter heard him calling. Herbert climbed out of the laundry basket, and Walter came out of Sunny's parents' wardrobe. The two of them looked for Violet, so that they could all go down together, but she did not seem to be in or under or behind anything in the flat, and she did not answer when they called her name.

'Perhaps she's already gone down,' said Walter. So the two friends went downstairs, hoping to find Violet there.

Following Walter into the shop, Herbert looked outside and said, 'The coach of bones has gone.'

'So's my wardrobe,' said Walter.

'Oh no!' said Herbert, seeing the strange space where Walter's wardrobe had been. Sunny came over, greeting them with relief. He explained that Walter's wardrobe had been sold to Mrs Prenderghast. 'There's still Abigail's wardrobe,' he added.

Walter said Abigail's wardrobe was very nice and would be just fine for him and Herbert.

'Where's Violet?' asked Sunny.

'We were hoping to find her down here,' said Walter.

'She's not down here,' said Sunny.

'She's not upstairs either,' said Walter.

'Perhaps she's gone for a walk,' said Herbert.

'Yes,' said Walter. 'She'll probably come through the door any minute now.'

Some hours later, when Violet had still not turned up, Walter said, 'If she's gone for a walk, it's a very long walk.' In the meantime, Sunny had been going to and fro between the shop and the flat: after doing his homework, and after his tea, and then again after his bath, he came downstairs wanting to know if Violet was back yet. Eventually, he suggested phoning their friends to see if they knew anything. They phoned the Hotel Splendid and spoke to Elsie, who was sorry to say she had no idea where Violet might be. They promised to let one another know as soon as they had news.

After hanging up, Sunny and the ghosts were quiet

for a moment, and then Herbert said, 'I expect Violet will roll in at midnight, having been at a dance hall.'

'That's probably it,' said Walter, hopefully.

Sunny was being called to bed, and Herbert and Walter said he should go and that by the time he woke up, Violet would no doubt be home.

When Sunny had gone up to bed, Herbert said to Walter, 'What worries me is that we haven't seen Violet since the coach of bones turned up.'

'But Violet came upstairs with us,' said Walter.

'Did she?' said Herbert, trying to think. 'Did you actually see her come upstairs?'

'Well, no,' admitted Walter.

'Nor did I,' said Herbert. 'We just assumed she was right behind us. What if Violet was still in the shop, out in the open, and the Wicked Lady got her and took her away in the coach of bones?'

'What are we going to do?' asked Walter, sitting down on the chaise longue and putting his ghostly head in his ghostly hands. Herbert sat down next to him and the two old friends stayed there thinking and worrying while the clocks ticked on and night descended.

CHAPTER THREE

The Wicked Lady

SUNNY WAS UP early. He went straight down to the shop, hoping to find that Violet had turned up overnight. He was disappointed to find that she had not.

'We think we might know what happened,' said Walter.

Herbert nodded. 'The Wicked Lady's been coming to the shop,' he said, 'each morning, before opening time.'

'We think she must have taken Violet,' said Walter.

This was a lot for Sunny to take in. 'So there really is a Wicked Lady?' he asked. 'And she's been coming here?'

'Yes,' said Herbert, 'in her coach of bones.'

'We both saw the coach of bones,' said Walter.

'And you think she's taken Violet?' asked Sunny.

'Yesterday morning, Violet was here, then the

Wicked Lady came, and now Violet's gone,' said Herbert.

Sunny was thinking. 'Perhaps the Wicked Lady will come again this morning,' he said.

'Yes,' said Herbert worriedly. 'She might come back to get me or Walter.'

'But we *want* her to come back,' said Sunny.

'Do we?' said Herbert, who really didn't.

'Yes,' said Sunny.

'Even though she's so scary?' said Herbert. 'Even though there's nothing in this whole world I'm more afraid of?'

'If we want to find out where Violet is,' said Sunny, 'we're going to have to talk to the Wicked Lady. You're going to have to face your fear.'

Sunny went back upstairs to get dressed and grab some breakfast, then waited in the shop with Herbert and Walter. Each time they heard traffic or footsteps approaching, they readied themselves, but the traffic and the footsteps passed by.

'What if she doesn't come?' asked Herbert.

'We just have to hope she does,' said Walter.

Sunny sat down at the cash desk, switched on the computer and worked quietly for a few minutes.

'What are you doing?' asked Walter.

'I'm making a poster,' said Sunny. He showed them what he had done:

HAVE YOU SEEN VIOLET VAN BRUGGEN?

LAST SEEN IN THE ANTIQUE SHOP

He added a contact number and printed out a dozen copies, while the Wicked Lady's usual arrival time came and went.

'She hasn't come,' said Herbert, and he realised that, despite his fear, he was disappointed, because there was nothing in the whole world he wanted more than to find Violet.

'I'll put these posters up on my way to school,' said Sunny.

The ghosts thought this was a good idea.

'We will find Violet,' said Sunny, although the look on his face said that he was not sure how.

When Sunny had gone out with the posters, Herbert and Walter waited some more on their own. Just before nine o'clock, they heard loud footsteps, but it was only Sunny's dad coming down to open the shop. He came in whistling, as if it were just an ordinary day. He unlocked the front door and turned the sign around to say OPEN. Herbert and Walter were wondering what on earth to do now, when they heard a clattering, rumbling, clip-clopping, rolling noise, and turned to the window just as the coach of bones came to a stop outside. They clung to one another, and watched as the carriage door opened and the Wicked Lady emerged. She stepped down onto the pavement and walked to the door of the shop, her shadowy gaze falling on Herbert and Walter, who were staring back, wide-eyed.

The door, though unlocked, was still closed, but the Wicked Lady walked through it as if it were not even there. Herbert's ghostly legs were trembling but he stood his ground, faced the Wicked Lady and said, with his ghostly voice shaking, 'What have you done with Violet?'

'Who's Violet?' enquired the Wicked Lady, surprising Herbert with a voice that was not as demonic as he had been expecting.

'Violet's our friend,' said Walter. 'We want to know where she is.'

'We know you were here yesterday morning,' said Herbert, 'when Violet went missing.'

'I did come here yesterday,' said the Wicked Lady. 'I've been coming each morning since Monday, but I'm afraid I don't know anything about your friend Violet.'

'If you didn't take Violet,' said Herbert, stepping out of the way of a middle-aged man coming into the shop with a fine set of old encyclopedias that he was hoping to sell, 'what were you doing here?'

'I came to find *you* actually,' said the Wicked Lady.

'I knew it,' said Herbert. 'I knew you were after me all along.'

'I heard you gossiping about me as you were leaving the castle and decided to come and have a word with you,' said the Wicked Lady. 'Having hesitated, I failed to catch you there, but luckily the name and address of this shop were printed on the side of your vehicle, so I knew where to find you. Except, when I arrived at the shop, you weren't here. I was so disappointed. But never mind, you're here now.'

'But Violet's not,' persisted Herbert.

'Hmm,' said the Wicked Lady, moving aside for an elderly couple who were heading for a display of fancy old hats. 'Where did you last see her?'

'Right here in the shop. Normally, she'd have been in the stationery cupboard,' said Herbert, pointing at it. 'But yesterday we were hiding . . .'

'Hiding?' said the Wicked Lady.

'From you,' admitted Herbert. When he saw how hurt she looked, he wished he hadn't said it.

'Oh,' said the Wicked Lady. 'I see.'

'We thought Violet was with us,' explained Walter, 'but she wasn't.'

'She wasn't in the stationery cupboard either,' said the Wicked Lady.

'How do you know?' asked Walter.

'Because I hid in there myself,' said the Wicked Lady. 'You see, while I was in the shop, still hoping to see you, a young man came in. I thought he might just be young enough to see me, so I hid in that cupboard. I watched through the keyhole so that I would know when it was safe to come out. He and the woman he was with took a while browsing and buying a wardrobe, so I was in the cupboard for quite a while. They didn't see me though, and I didn't see your friend.'

'Perhaps Violet was hiding somewhere else,' said Herbert.

'Did you say those two customers bought a wardrobe?' asked Walter.

'Yes,' said the Wicked Lady. 'They were from a museum – that's what they wanted the wardrobe for. It was odd though: when the shopkeeper was in the room, the woman and the young man were very complimentary about the wardrobe. They said it was perfect.'

'It *is* a lovely wardrobe,' said Walter fondly.

'But when the shopkeeper left the room and couldn't hear what they were saying, they were very rude about the wardrobe, as if they didn't think very much of it at all. I heard them call it cheap junk.'

Walter looked cross.

'I thought perhaps they'd changed their minds about buying it,' said the Wicked Lady, 'but when the shopkeeper came back – with a key, to lock the wardrobe door – they started being all nice about it again. Anyway, they bought it and took it away in their vehicle.'

Walter said to Herbert, 'If Violet didn't come upstairs with us to hide, and was still down here when the Wicked Lady arrived, do you think it's possible she might, at the last minute, have hidden in my wardrobe?'

Herbert's ghostly jaw dropped. 'And when the people from the museum took the wardrobe away, they accidentally took Violet away as well.'

Walter said to the Wicked Lady, 'I don't suppose you know which museum they were from, do you?'

'I know it's not the Museum of Dartmoor Life,' said the Wicked Lady. 'It's a brand-new museum. The woman left a telephone number.' The Wicked Lady went to the cash desk, opened the ledger and showed them the number next to Mrs Prenderghast's name.

While Sunny's dad was showing a customer a selection of music boxes, Herbert picked up the phone, dialled the number and waited until someone at the other end said, 'Museum of the Weird, how may I help?'

'Museum of the Weird?' said Herbert, puzzled.

'Hello?' said the person at the other end of the line. 'Hello?'

Herbert put the phone down. He sat down at the computer and googled 'Museum of the Weird'. 'Right,' he said, 'I've got the address. We could get there in half an hour in the van.'

'But how can we ask for the van when Sunny's at school?' said Walter.

'Hmm,' said Herbert. 'Perhaps I could drive the van.'

'I don't think that's a good idea,' said Walter. 'You're not insured.'

'That's right,' said Herbert. 'I would need insurance.' He started googling insurance companies, hoping to find one that would agree to insure a ghost to drive a van, but when he tried to phone them he realised that the problem with this plan was that the person who answered could not hear him.

'I know,' said Herbert. 'We'll write a letter to

Sunny's parents, explaining the situation and asking if we can have a lift in the van.' There was a pad of paper open on the desk, and Herbert said that he would dictate the letter and Walter could write it.

'*Dear Sunny's mother and father . . .*' began Herbert.

'Hang on,' said Walter, who had not yet finished writing the address and the date in the top right-hand corner of the page. When he had done that, he said to Herbert, 'All right, go on.'

'*Hello,*' continued Herbert, '*how are you? We are ghosts. Our names are Walter and Herbert. We haven't met. I don't mean Walter and I haven't met: we met quite a while ago, in the New Year I think it was, and we know one another quite well now. No, I mean the two of us haven't met the two of you. Well, in a way we have – we're in the same room quite a lot of the time – but although we've seen you, you've never seen us, so I think I would have to say that technically we, Walter and I, have not met you, Sunny's mother and father. We live . . . No . . . We reside downstairs, in the shop, in the wardrobe and the blanket box respectively – well, we did until these items of furniture were recently sold, which, in fact, is why we are now writing.*'

'Wait up,' said Walter. 'I'm still on *in the New Year.*'

Herbert waited patiently for him to catch up, and just as Walter turned to him, ready for the next line, Sunny's dad came over to the cash desk with a brimful mug which he put down on the pad of paper without really looking, slopping tea onto the paragraph that Walter had just written.

Walter sighed.

'Maybe we don't need the van,' said Herbert. 'We could cycle there. It would take a bit longer but all we'd need is a bicycle, and another bicycle.'

But they did not have any bicycles.

When the Wicked Lady spoke, Herbert and Walter jumped – they had almost forgotten that she was still there.

'Why don't I take you there,' she said, 'in my coach of bones?'

CHAPTER FOUR

The Prenderghasts

The Wicked Lady's dog had been waiting for her outside the shop. When it saw her coming out, it wagged its ghostly tail and she patted its ghostly head. The Wicked Lady and Herbert and Walter climbed into the coach of bones, and the dog jumped in with them. When everyone was safely inside, the phantom horses set off.

Neither Herbert nor Walter had ever travelled in a supernatural vehicle before. They were used to the van, which had to stop at traffic lights and got stuck in traffic jams, but when the Wicked Lady said, 'Hold tight,' the coach of bones went right through whatever was in their way. It did make Herbert feel a bit sick but all he really cared about was getting to the museum and finding Violet.

Leaving the coach of bones parked in the street – attended by its driver and guarded by the spectral black dog – Herbert, Walter and the Wicked Lady went on foot down a narrow alleyway, at the end of which stood the museum. The building was small and drab, with a sign over the door saying MUSEUM OF THE WEIRD.

'Even if Mrs Prenderghast is here,' said Herbert, 'I don't know how we're going to communicate with her.' He opened the door and peered into the dingy foyer. He could see a ticket desk, but as the museum was not yet open to the public, there was nobody behind it. The ghosts went into the foyer and the door closed behind them.

Ahead of them was an archway, beyond which they found the exhibition area. The walls were lined with display cases housing captioned photographs and labelled artifacts and eyewitness accounts of encounters with aliens and sightings of creatures such as Bigfoot, the Abominable Snowman and the Loch Ness Monster.

They could not see Walter's wardrobe anywhere, but there were some big display cases that were still empty and they supposed it would be put into one of them.

'I can hear someone talking,' whispered the Wicked Lady. They all stood quietly and listened. The Wicked Lady moved towards a door marked OFFICE and poked her head through it. When she pulled it back out, she turned to Herbert and Walter and said, 'The people who bought the wardrobe are in there.'

Walter took a look himself. He saw a middle-aged woman sitting behind a desk, talking to a young man who had his back to the door. 'We need to get it into its display case,' Mrs Prenderghast was saying. 'You'll have to do it, and you'll have to be careful. I want it done today. It will be the star attraction at our grand opening next week. We need to get people in here, buying tickets, spending their money. Just think how much they'd pay to see something like that.'

The young man said, 'I'll get the wardrobe out of the storeroom before lunch.'

Walter liked his wardrobe a lot, but as far as he could see it was very ordinary, not at all weird, so he did not really understand why the Museum of the Weird wanted it or why people would pay to come and see it inside a display case. But he could not waste time wondering about that: what was important was finding Violet. Walter withdrew from the office and said to the others, 'The wardrobe's in the storeroom.'

They looked around. In the foyer, near the empty ticket desk, they found a door with STOREROOM written on it. The door was locked, but Walter and the Wicked Lady could go through it. Walter said to Herbert, 'We'll just go and look for my wardrobe and see if Violet got locked in there by accident.'

The storeroom was quite small and tidy, so it was not hard to find Walter's wardrobe, which was next to Herbert's blanket box. Walter put his head through the wardrobe door, saying, 'Violet? Are you in here?'

'Walter!' said Violet. 'Oh, I'm so pleased to see you. I can't get out.'

Walter was delighted to have found her. 'We've been ever so worried about you,' he said. 'We thought the Wicked Lady must have taken you. Then Herbert realised you might have got accidentally locked in the wardrobe that Mrs Prenderghast bought.'

'Yes,' said Violet, 'I did get locked in, but it wasn't an accident. It's not the wardrobe she wanted – it's me.'

'You?' said Walter. 'You mean, she knows you're in here?'

'Yes,' said Violet. 'She wants to exhibit me in the museum. When they were in the shop, looking at furniture, they were really looking for ghosts. The young man, who's her son, saw me in the wardrobe. He locked the door so I couldn't escape, and they brought me here. I've asked very nicely to be let out, and not so nicely, and, most recently, not nicely at all, but nothing I say does any good.'

'She wants to exhibit you?' said Walter, horrified. 'We've got to get you out of here.'

'Yes please,' said Violet. 'Can you see the key?'

Walter looked around for the key, and the Wicked

44

Lady helped him, but they could not see it anywhere. Walter, scratching his ghostly head, had a think. He could get into the wardrobe but Violet could not get out, so that was no use. He could get out of the storeroom but only without the wardrobe and without Violet. He would have to go looking for the keys, to unlock the wardrobe and the storeroom door. Now that he knew Mrs Prenderghast's fiendish plan, he was not exactly keen to encounter her or her son, but if he was going to help Violet, he was going to have to take that risk.

While Walter and the Wicked Lady were in the storeroom with Violet, Herbert was looking around. He read the information leaflets in the foyer, and straightened a picture that was hanging on the wall, and browsed the display cases in the exhibition area. The big, empty ones were unlocked, their glass doors standing open, ready to receive their exhibits.

He could hear the clip-clopping of Mrs Prenderghast's high heels as she came out of the office and into the exhibition area, saying to the young man, 'Which display case shall we put it in?' They approached the empty display cases in front of which Herbert was standing. 'I'll write a description to go with it. I'll think up some exotic story that will capture people's imaginations.'

The young man had stopped in his tracks and was staring at Herbert. 'It's you,' he said. 'You're the ghost from the blanket box.'

Herbert was gobsmacked. 'You can see me?' he said.

'Yes,' said the young man, approaching him, 'I can see you.'

'But grown-ups can't normally see me,' said Herbert.

'I'm seventeen,' said the young man, coming still closer. 'Nearly eighteen.'

'Who are you talking to, Edgar?' said Mrs Prenderghast, looking where he was looking but seeing no one there.

'It's the first ghost,' said Edgar to his mother. 'The one I saw in the blanket box in the junk shop.'

Mrs Prenderghast looked thrilled. 'When you came home and told me what you'd seen, I was so excited,' she said. Her look turned darker. 'And then, when I brought the blanket box here and you opened it up and told me it was empty, I was so disappointed.'

Edgar was now inches away from Herbert. 'Soon,' Edgar said to him, 'I expect I won't be able to see you any more, but it won't matter, I'll know where you are.'

'In the antique shop?' said Herbert.

'No,' said Edgar, pressing in so close that Herbert instinctively took a step backwards and, to his surprise, landed on his ghostly bottom. By the time he realised that what had tripped him up was the base of the display case, and that he was now *inside* the display case, Edgar was shutting the door, saying, 'You'll be here, in our collection of ghosts.'

Mrs Prenderghast stepped forward with a big bunch of keys, like a jailer's keyring, and while Herbert struggled to his feet and reached for the door, Mrs Prenderghast slipped the key into the lock and turned it.

Edgar watched Herbert banging on the toughened glass and demanding – in a muffled voice – to be let out, and then he turned to his mother with a smile and the two of them walked away.

Violet had been locked inside Walter's wardrobe since Tuesday morning, and now it was Wednesday and nearly lunchtime. It was a very long time to spend locked inside a wardrobe. *It could be worse though,* she was thinking. *At least Walter keeps his wardrobe nice and clean, and his winter coat is very comfortable.*

It could be a lot worse, if nobody knew where I was, if Walter wasn't here to help. It could be so much worse, if—

'I'm going to get you . . .' said the Wicked Lady, putting her head and shoulders through the wardrobe door.

Violet screamed.

The Wicked Lady looked taken aback. 'Sorry,' she said, 'I didn't mean to startle you. I was just saying, I'm going to get you home, dear, in my coach of bones, just as soon as we can find the keys to get you out of here.'

'Sorry,' said Walter, his face appearing beside the Wicked Lady's. 'I should have introduced you. Violet, this is the Wicked Lady. She's been a great help. She's going to stay with you while I go out to look for the keys.'

Violet looked with embarrassment at the Wicked Lady and said, 'I'm so sorry I screamed in your face.'

'That's quite all right, dear,' said the Wicked Lady.

Walter left the storeroom, wondering where the keys might be kept. He decided to look in the office, and was halfway across the foyer when Mrs Prenderghast and the young man came out of the exhibition area. 'They don't seem able to go through walls,' the young man was saying. 'I suppose they can only do that in storybooks.'

'That's lucky for us,' said Mrs Prenderghast.

'Of course,' said the young man, 'grown-ups won't be able to see them.'

'No,' agreed Mrs Prenderghast, 'but we'll charge children to see them *and* the grown-ups who'll have to bring them. I'm ready for my lunch now. You can go and fetch the other ghost.'

'There's another one!' said the young man.

'Of course there's another one,' said Mrs Prenderghast. 'The one in the storeroom.'

'No,' said the young man, staring across the foyer at Walter, 'there's *another* one!'

'Where on earth are they all coming from?' wondered Mrs Prenderghast.

'Young man,' said Walter. 'You've got my friend locked in a wardrobe and I'd really like you to let her out so that we can go home.'

'Let it out?' said the young man. 'Let it out, when we've gone to all the trouble of getting it here? No, we're going to put it on display, next to the first one.'

'The first one?' said Walter.

'The old man one.'

'Herbert? You mean you've got Herbert? Now look here . . .' said Walter sternly.

'I want this one too,' said Mrs Prenderghast.

The young man took a step towards Walter.

Walter fled, hurrying back across the foyer, around

a corner and into the storeroom, where he told the Wicked Lady what had happened. 'I used my sternest voice,' said Walter, 'but it did no good at all.'

'I think,' said the Wicked Lady, 'we might need a different tactic.'

Leaving Edgar to capture the ghost he had encountered in the foyer, and to get it and the ghost they had in the storeroom into the display cases, Mrs Prenderghast returned to the office to eat her lunch. She sat down at her desk with her sandwich and set about making up a little description for each ghost. **Here you see**, she typed, **the restless spirit of . . .** She paused, and then continued: **. . . a cruel and callous squire, who cheated his brother . . .** Without turning her head from her work, she reached for her sandwich, which was not where she expected it to be. She looked around and saw it on the opposite side of the desk. She blinked at it. Once again, she reached for it, but when her fingers were almost touching it, it moved away. She stared at her sandwich, as if what had just happened could not possibly have happened. For the third time, she aimed her hand at her sandwich, but before she could grab it, it scooted away from her, flying right off the desk and onto the floor.

'Edgar!' she called. 'Edgar!'

Her son, coming in, said, 'Yes, Mother?'

'Edgar,' said Mrs Prenderghast. 'Is that ghost in here?'

Edgar looked around. 'No, Mother,' he said.

Walter, who had quickly hidden himself in a cupboard, smiled to himself.

Edgar noticed the sandwich that was lying on the floor, picked it up and handed it to his mother.

'I think my desk slopes,' said Mrs Prenderghast. 'I'll have to get a new one.'

Edgar left the office and Mrs Prenderghast eyed her sandwich. Her stomach growled. She leaned forward, opening her mouth to take a bite. Her teeth gnashed together, with nothing in between them. The sandwich that had been in her hands was once again on the floor.

'Edgar!' she called. 'Edgar!'

That tufty-haired ghost had given Edgar the slip. With all the doors closed, it seemed to Edgar that the ghost must be trapped in the foyer or the exhibition area, and yet he had looked everywhere and had not found it. It was not behind the ticket desk, and it was not behind the coat stand. Looking around the display cases, Edgar complained through the glass to Herbert about all the trouble the ghosts were causing him, and how cross his mother would be if any one of them escaped.

Giving up his search for the time being, he said to Herbert, 'I'm going to go and get the frizzy-haired one out of storage.' Edgar made his way out of the exhibition area, patting his pockets. He would need to fetch the keys, which were kept by his mother, who, in fact, he could hear calling for him. He was crossing the foyer when he froze in surprise and alarm. There, only metres away from him, was a spectral black dog, and it was looking his way. It bared its fangs and growled at him. Edgar edged towards the office, but the snarling hound moved too, blocking his way. Edgar decided to make a run for it, but when he bolted towards the front door, the dog gave chase. It pursued him out of the building and down the narrow alleyway, towards what ought to have been a perfectly normal street and a little bit of lunchtime traffic. Instead, at the end of the alleyway, Edgar came face to skeletal face with a pair of phantom horses whose reins were held by a head-less driver who sat atop a coach built from bones and decorated with skulls. Edgar shrieked and the horses snorted; the horses reared and Edgar ran. He ran and ran, down street after street, hearing the hooves and the rattling bones just behind him. Whenever he stopped – to catch his breath or to hide – the coach of bones stopped alongside him and the carriage door began to open, and Edgar ran on.

Mrs Prenderghast had been trying to eat her sandwich all afternoon. She had chased it all around the office. She had tried creeping up on it and running at it and pouncing on it. She had tried ignoring it and then taking it by surprise. But it had defeated her. She had called and called for Edgar, but he had not come; she had no idea where he was. In the end, she went home, but there too she found that she was unable to eat anything. The food simply would not stay on her fork or her plate, or the fork would not stay in her hand, or the plate would not stay on the table. In the end, she went to bed hungry.

Wearily, she lay her head on her pillow and closed her eyes. But she could not sleep: she could feel something blowing in her ear. Opening her eyes again, she saw that the window was wide open, so she got up and closed it. She got back into bed, sighing as she lay down to try again to sleep, and found that her pillow had gone. Determined to sleep with or without her pillow, she squeezed her eyes shut, but within moments she was opening them again: someone was knocking on the front door.

Mrs Prenderghast sat up and put her feet in her slippers, which were full of jam. When she had got at least some of the jam out of her slippers, she made her way downstairs, calling, 'Edgar? Is that you?' but when she opened the door, she could see no one there. Quite exhausted now, she returned to her bed and lay down, putting her head on a cactus. When she had moved the cactus, she closed her eyes, and felt something blowing in her ear.

Finally, she gave up trying to sleep and went yawning into the kitchen to try at least to make a cup of instant coffee. It was still dark outside. She could see her reflection in the window: she looked rather pale, and had dark circles under her eyes caused by her sleepless night. She put the kettle on to boil and took a mug off the mug tree. She opened the jar of coffee granules and spooned some out, then flung them across the room. She took a deep breath and tried again: she put the spoon into the jar, brought out a heap of coffee granules, and flung them across the room. Gazing longingly at her empty mug, she raised her arm and hit herself on the head with the spoon. In the meantime, the kettle had boiled and the steam had covered the kitchen window in condensation. Words were forming in the condensation, and the words said *LET MY FRIENDS GO.*

Mrs Prenderghast left the house in haste, still in her nightie. She went directly to the museum. After unlocking the storeroom and Violet's wardrobe, she hurried into the exhibition area and unlocked Herbert's display case. Finally, she opened the door that led from the museum into the alleyway, and waited in the foyer until the door slammed itself shut.

Walter, Herbert and Violet were ten minutes into what was going to be a long walk home – it was dawn and they did not expect to be back at the shop until lunchtime – when the coach of bones rumbled to a stop beside them.

'Hop in,' said the Wicked Lady. 'I'll give you a lift home.'

'I *am* pleased to see you,' said Herbert, climbing

aboard. There was a limit, he thought, to how far one could be expected to walk in slippers.

'Where's Edgar?' asked Walter.

'When I last saw him,' said the Wicked Lady, 'he was running into the sea.'

'I don't know what we'd have done without you,' said Walter.

'Thank you so much,' said Violet, who was excited to have her first ever ride in the coach of bones.

'Seeing as we have transport,' said Herbert, 'do you think we could pay a visit to our friends at the Hotel Splendid before going home? They've been just as worried as us about Violet going missing. It would be nice to drop in and let them know we've found her.'

'Of course,' said the Wicked Lady. They set off. 'Are they the three ghosts I saw you with at the castle?' she asked.

'Yes,' said Herbert, 'and Abigail, who couldn't come that day.'

'Abigail is "the ghost that haunts the Hotel Splendid",' explained Violet.

'Is she being punished for something she did in her life?' asked the Wicked Lady.

'Oh no,' said Violet. 'It's just a role she plays.' She told the Wicked Lady about the spooky performances at the hotel, and all the people who came to stay there.

'You mean, the ghosts are *seen?*' said the Wicked Lady. 'And people still come?'

'Oh yes,' said Violet. 'People come hoping to see the ghosts or at least the ghostly goings-on.'

'Aren't they scared?' asked the Wicked Lady.

'They *are* a bit scared,' said Violet, 'but at the same time they seem to enjoy it.'

While the phantom horses galloped on, the Wicked Lady sat gazing thoughtfully out of the window.

At the Hotel Splendid, Herbert introduced the Wicked Lady to the resident ghosts, including Abigail, who was back from London, thrilled to have had the opportunity to perform in a West End theatre but glad to be home. While Abigail made a fuss of the spectral black dog, the ghosts explained what had happened, starting with Herbert seeing the Wicked Lady at the castle.

The Wicked Lady explained that she normally stayed out of sight. 'I know I scare people,' she said, 'especially children, and I'd rather not. Unless they deserve it, like the Prenderghasts. I have nowhere else to go though. My home was demolished hundreds of years ago. The castle, which belonged to my family, might be in ruins, but there's nowhere else I belong, nowhere I feel wanted. After the first few hundred years, I did start to feel rather lonely. All those visitors and no one to talk to. My driver's very sweet, he loves those horses, but he's not a big talker, being headless. When I saw you, I hoped that, being ghosts, you wouldn't be scared of me, and that, having heads, you might speak to me.' The Wicked Lady looked at Herbert. 'After I heard you talking,' she said, 'I wanted to explain that not everything you've been told about me is true.'

The Hotel Splendid ghosts heard about her visits to the shop, and were shocked to learn about the kidnappings, ('The rotters!' exclaimed Elsie), and delighted by the details of the escape ('Bravo!' said Mary). And then, added Herbert, the Wicked Lady had been kind enough to bring them here. Abigail, tickling the spectral dog's ears, said, 'I do hope you'll stay to see this afternoon's performance.'

So the Wicked Lady stayed, and watched the matinee with interest. She saw the rocking of the chair, and the ringing of the bell, and the playing of the pump organ, and the flickering of the lights, and the ghost that haunts the Hotel Splendid wailing and moaning and disappearing through the wall, and she saw for herself how the guests, despite being scared, were thrilled by the idea of being in a haunted hotel.

When it was time to leave, Elsie, Mary, Abigail and Alan thanked the Wicked Lady for visiting, and for helping their friends. 'Thank you for helping me as well,' said the Wicked Lady, though the Hotel Splendid ghosts had no idea what she meant.

Travelling back to the antique shop in the coach of bones, Violet said to the Wicked Lady, 'So, you were saying, the stories that are told about you aren't true?'

'It's almost all made up,' said the Wicked Lady. She told them about her life: her birth in the summer of 1596, when Elizabeth I was on the throne; being orphaned at the age of nine and inheriting the family fortune; her first husband, 'who,' she said, looking at Herbert, 'I did not marry for money. Mostly, my husbands married *me* for money.'

Her first husband, she explained, died from a fever. She married again. Her second husband died a few months later. She married again, and again. 'I outlived each one of my husbands, but that doesn't mean I killed them all. That's the story that's told about me though, and so I'm doomed to spend my afterlife in purgatory, riding across the moor each night in my coach of bones.'

Violet, Herbert and Walter were very sorry to hear this. When the Wicked Lady had dropped them off outside the antique shop, and when they had waved her off, calling, 'Goodbye,' and, 'Thank you,' and, 'It was very nice to meet you,' Violet said to Herbert and Walter, 'I wish there was some way we could help her in return.'

Inside the shop, they were surprised and delighted to see – filling what had recently been horribly empty spaces – Herbert's blanket box and Walter's wardrobe.

When, a little while later, Sunny came home from school, he was even more surprised and delighted to discover the blanket box and Herbert inside it, and Walter's wardrobe with Walter inside it, and Violet safe and well inside the stationery cupboard, popping some bubblewrap. 'You're home!' said Sunny. 'I'm so glad to see you!' Violet was very glad to see him too, and they did their best to hug one another. 'But where have you been?' asked Sunny. 'And how come the furniture's back?'

The ghosts told Sunny everything that had happened, and Herbert said what a horrible experience it had been being trapped in the display case to be exhibited at the Museum of the Weird. He stomped indignantly about the shop in his ghostly pyjamas, saying, 'I'm not weird.'

Sunny's mum explained that Mrs Prenderghast had arrived in her van, on the dot of opening time, keen to return both items of furniture, which had not been to her liking after all. 'She didn't want her money back though,' said Sunny's mum. 'She wouldn't even come into the shop. She just wanted to get rid of the furniture and get away as quickly as she could. And when I said I'd phone if we got anything else she might want in the museum, she said, "Please don't."'

'That's strange,' said Sunny's dad.

'Very strange,' said Sunny's mum.

CHAPTER FIVE

The Haunted Castle

VIOLET HAD BEEN hard at work for weeks. She was writing a new book and it was nearly finished.

While Violet was at her writing desk, finishing off a paragraph, Sunny was upstairs in the kitchen, packing his rucksack for a school trip. His class was visiting Okehampton Castle and he was looking forward to the outing. He put his water bottle and his snack and his lunch into his rucksack and zipped it up.

'Have you got everything you need?' asked his mum.

'Yes,' said Sunny, 'I think so.'

He said goodbye to his parents and went downstairs, greeting the ghosts as he passed through the shop. Walter was putting away the box of games, and Violet was putting away her sheaf of papers, and Herbert was fetching the key to the stationery cupboard.

'See you later!' said Sunny.

'See you later!' called the ghosts. 'Have a good day!'

Just after nine o'clock, the coach collected the schoolchildren and set off for the medieval ruins. Sunny was sitting next to his friend Charlie, who had never been to Okehampton Castle, so Sunny told him what was there, 'and it's haunted by the Wicked Lady,' he added.

Charlie rolled his eyes and said, 'That's just a story. Ghosts aren't real.'

'She is real,' insisted Sunny. But he could see that Charlie did not believe him, and he knew that even if the Wicked Lady was there, she would not show herself.

At the castle, they were taken on a tour of the site, walking in a group through what remained of the barbican and the gatehouse and the guard room, and from there up some steps to the roofless Great Hall, beyond which were the kitchens and the lodgings and the chapel and the keep. All the while, Sunny looked and looked for the Wicked Lady, while Charlie teased him about his imaginary friend.

It was as they were leaving the chapel that Sunny thought he saw, out of the corner of his eye, a figure in the distance, moving between the ruins. He turned his head, but there was no one there, and none of the others seemed to have noticed.

After lunch, the class went off in twos and threes to sketch the ruins. Sunny sat with Charlie, and was concentrating so hard on his shading that he didn't notice anyone approaching until a ghostly voice said, 'Hello.' Sunny looked up into the shadowy eyes of the Wicked Lady.

'You're here!' said Sunny. 'Charlie, look, it's the Wicked Lady.' But Charlie had already seen her and was staring at her, with his mouth wide open.

The Wicked Lady was pressed against the stony wall, as if she were playing hide-and-seek. 'This is fun!' she said. Then, seeing Sunny's puzzlement, she explained: 'I overheard what you said the first time you came to the castle. You said you were disappointed you didn't see me. I've been thinking about that. And I met your friends at the Hotel Splendid and saw how much the guests enjoyed the idea of being in a haunted hotel. I wouldn't want to really terrify my visitors, but I have been trying out some gentle haunting, letting myself be glimpsed among the ruins. It seems to be going down quite well.' Going up on tiptoe, she peeped over the wall.

A little voice in the distance said, 'I can see a ghost!'

The Wicked Lady ducked back down.

Lots of little voices in the distance said, 'Where?

. . . There's no ghost . . . I can't see any ghost . . . There's no such thing as ghosts . . .'

Sunny grinned at the Wicked Lady. 'I was hoping I'd see you,' he said. 'I know Violet and Herbert and Walter would love to see you too. Perhaps you could come to the shop one night?'

The Wicked Lady sighed and said, 'I wish I could, but every night I'm compelled to ride across the moor, taking a single blade of grass from the castle to my birthplace, and I must do this until I have plucked each and every blade of grass, by which time it will be the end of the world. As much as I would love to see my friends, I am doomed to spend an eternity of nights riding across the moor, in my ghastly coach of bones.'

'Why?' asked Sunny.

'Obviously, I would *rather* travel in a vehicle that's not made out of human bones,' said the Wicked Lady. 'I wouldn't mind a sporty little car – a cherry-red Mini would be nice – but this coach of bones with which I'm burdened reflects the crimes of which I'm accused.'

Sunny could see that it was a pretty good vehicle for doing penance in. 'But I mean,' he said, 'why do you have to do penance at all? Violet told me you didn't do all the things you're said to have done.'

'But I'm *believed* to have done them,' said the Wicked Lady. 'I'll be in purgatory until I can clear my name.'

'Oh,' said Sunny thoughtfully.

The Wicked Lady, hearing children nearby, said, 'Do excuse me. I'd better go and do some haunting.' She emerged from her hiding place and walked openly between the ruins.

'There!' said a little voice. 'I see her!'

Sunny bent over his drawing again, and sketched her in.

Back home, in between teatime and bedtime, Sunny went down to the shop to say goodnight to the ghosts. Herbert was climbing out of his blanket box, and Walter came out of his wardrobe, and Violet was ready to come out of the stationery cupboard.

'Did you have a good time at the castle?' asked Walter.

Sunny said he'd had a great time. 'I even saw the Wicked Lady. So did Charlie. He told his mum and she was really excited: she said she'd heard the story of the Wicked Lady but had no idea she was real.'

'Come and sit with me,' said Violet, 'and tell me everything that happened. Start at the beginning.'

They sat together on the chaise longue, and Sunny said, 'The coach left school just after nine o'clock.'

'Who did you sit next to?' asked Violet.

They talked until it was time for Sunny to go upstairs to bed, and then Violet sat down at her writing desk to work on the final chapter of her book: she wrote about Sunny and Charlie visiting the castle and seeing the Wicked Lady, and when she wrote about the Wicked Lady saying, 'I *would love to see my friends,*' she smiled, and when she wrote, '*I'll be in purgatory until I can clear my name,*' she paused, thinking.

The following morning, when Sunny passed through the shop on his way to school, he found Violet waiting for him. She was holding some pages, covered in her neatest handwriting.

'Sunny,' she said, 'Charlie's mum's a historian, isn't she? You told me she's interested in local people's stories and gives talks about them. I was wondering if she'd be interested in this.'

'What is it?' asked Sunny.

'It's the story of the Wicked Lady,' said Violet, 'in her own words.'

'I'm *sure* she'll be interested,' said Sunny. He put the pages into his rucksack and promised to pass them on.

A few weeks later, Sunny was woken in the small hours by what sounded like a big old sing-along taking place downstairs. He picked up his night light and went out of his room and down to the antique shop, where he was surprised to find – sitting and standing around the piano, singing 'Yellow Submarine' – not three but four ghosts: Herbert, Walter, Violet and the Wicked Lady.

When the ghosts saw Sunny standing in the doorway and realised they had woken him up, they stopped singing and playing. Sunny, looking in confusion at the Wicked Lady, said, 'It's the middle of the night.'

The ghosts looked embarrassed and said, 'Sorry, Sunny.'

'We didn't mean to wake you up,' said the Wicked Lady.

'It's all right,' Sunny told her. 'But I mean, it's the middle of the night, when you're normally out on the moor taking blades of grass from one place to another. How come you're here?'

The Wicked Lady smiled and said she wanted to thank him for passing her story on to Charlie's mum, who had used it to give a series of talks, one of which took place at Okehampton Castle, where many people heard it, 'including me,' she added. 'Now that my true story is being told, I'm at peace. I can leave the grass to grow, and my nights are free.'

'You only get one afterlife,' said Walter. 'You might as well make the most of it.'

Sunny could see the coach of bones parked outside the shop, and asked the Wicked Lady if her driver might like to come in. Or, he wondered, might he like a cup of tea to keep him warm? But no, he realised, the driver was a ghost and would not be able to drink tea. Or, he suggested, would he like a book to read? But no, he realised, the driver was headless and would not be able to read a book. But the Wicked Lady assured Sunny that the driver preferred to stay with his horses and that he was quite all right as he was.

From then on, the Wicked Lady came regularly to the shop to see her new friends, and sometimes she stayed all night. She taught Violet and Herbert how to go through doors, and she taught Walter a Spanish dance, and she learnt to play Ludo and Snap and *Guess Who?*. They did try to keep the noise down though, and sometimes they went out and about in the coach of bones. Having read the information leaflets in the

foyer of the museum, Herbert had some suggestions for places to go and things to do. They visited Tintagel Castle, where King Arthur was said to have been born, and they argued about whether King Arthur had been real and whether the stories that were told about him were true. They borrowed a set of golf clubs from the antique shop and played a few rounds on a crazy golf course. They went canoeing, with Herbert and Walter in one canoe and Violet and the Wicked Lady in another. They considered going to the zoo, but none of them really felt like looking at animals in cages and enclosures. They visited their friends at the Hotel Splendid, and, when the tide was out, they went down to the beach. Abigail played fetch with the spectral black dog, and they all had a go at surfing, at which the Wicked Lady turned out to be unexpectedly good.

And sometimes, it was just the three of them, quite content to sit through the night in the comfort of the antique shop. At times, they still woke Sunny up playing music or laughing too loudly and he would come down in his pyjamas to say hello, and at other times it was deathly quiet, apart from the click of a multicoloured biro, the waft of a page being turned, the ticking of the clocks on the wall above the piano, and the sound of two ghostly friends playing Jenga.

An acrostic for the Wicked Lady

The clattering of ancient bones and
Horses' hooves upon the road has
Echoed through the centuries and
We've been trembling at the knees.
In ballads, books and now on blogs, a
Campfire tale of fiend and dog is
Kept alive from year to year and
Even other ghosts have feared the
Dreaded lady coming near.
Lately, though, she came this way
And stopped her coach outside to say
Do please step in with me and ride. Oh
Yes! her spooky friends replied.

Also by Alison Moore
Illustrated by Ross Collins

Sunny and the Ghosts
978-1-78463-126-0

Sunny and the Hotel Splendid
978-1-78463-202-1

This book has been typeset by
SALT PUBLISHING LIMITED
using Neacademia, a font designed by Sergei Egorov
for the Rosetta Type Foundry in the Czech Republic. It
is manufactured using Holmen Book Cream 70gsm, a
Forest Stewardship Council™ certified paper from the
Hallsta Paper Mill in Sweden. It was printed and bound
by Clays Limited in Bungay, Suffolk, Great Britain.

CROMER
GREAT BRITAIN
MMXX